Our Emotions and Behavior

But What If?

Sue Graves

Illustrated by
Desideria Guicciardini

free spirit
PUBLISHING®

Mom, Dad, and Daisy were moving to a new house. Daisy was going to a new school, too.

Mom and Dad said it was **very exciting.**

1

But Daisy wasn't excited at all.
She was **worried.**

What if she didn't like the new house? And **what if** the neighbors were mean?

3

Daisy was also worried about her cat, Tigger.

4

What if Tigger **didn't like** the new house? What if he ran away?

Daisy worried about her new school, too. She liked Miss Lane, her teacher. What if her new teacher **wasn't nice?**

And what if she didn't make any new friends? Daisy was **very worried.**

One night, Mom and Dad went out. Grandpa came to stay with Daisy. But when it was bedtime, Daisy couldn't sleep.

She told Grandpa about the new house.
She told him **all her** worries.

9

Then Grandpa said that when **he** was a boy, he **worried** about lots of things. He said he worried that he wasn't as tall as his friends.

Daisy laughed. Grandpa was very tall.
He was just as tall as Dad.

Grandpa said, "It's easy to worry about new things or big changes. And even if one or two of your worries come true at first, someone will be there to help you **solve the problem."**

13

Grandpa said it didn't help to worry about something that **might never happen.** He said it was better to look on the bright side.

Grandpa said Daisy might **love** her new house. Her new neighbors might be **really nice.**

15

Grandpa said Daisy's new school might be **even better** than her old one. Her new teacher might be **even nicer** than Miss Lane.

He said he thought she would make lots
of **new friends,** too.
Daisy felt **much better.**

Then Grandpa said he did not believe Tigger would ever run away. He said Tigger loved Daisy too much to do that!

Daisy felt **much, much better.**

19

Daisy went to bed. She fell fast asleep.
Best of all, she **didn't feel worried** anymore!

21

Can you tell the story of Levi going to his friend's birthday party?

How do you think Levi felt when he arrived?
How do you think he felt after he met his friend?

A note about sharing this book

The **Our Emotions and Behavior** series has been developed to provide a starting point for further discussion about children's feelings and behavior, in relation both to themselves and to other people.

But What If?
This story explores in a reassuring way some of the typical worries that children may experience. It also points out that different things worry different people and that not everyone worries about the same things.

The book aims to encourage children to have a developing awareness of their own needs, views, and feelings, and to be sensitive to the needs, views, and feelings of others.

Picture story
The picture story on pages 22 and 23 provides an opportunity for speaking and listening. Children are encouraged to tell the story illustrated in the panels: Levi is worried about going to his friend's birthday party. He is worried that he won't know many people. But he soon sees his friend and has fun joining in with the party games.

How to use the book
The book is designed for adults to share with either an individual child or a group of children, and as a starting point for discussion.

The book also provides visual support and repeated words and phrases to build confidence in children who are starting to read on their own.

Before reading the story
Choose a time to read when you and the children are relaxed and have time to share the story.

Spend time looking at the illustrations and discussing what the book may be about before reading it together.

After reading, talk about the book with the children

- What was the story about? Have any of the children ever moved? How did they feel? Were they worried about living in a new neighborhood? Were they worried about sleeping in a different bedroom? Were they worried that they might find it hard to make new friends, and were they upset at leaving old friends behind? Invite the children to tell you how they resolved their worries and who helped them.

  Ask if any of their worries turned out to be true. Also ask if they had worried about any things that did not happen. Encourage the children to talk about their experiences.

- Extend this discussion by talking about other things that worry the children. Take the opportunity to point out that different things worry different people and that not everyone worries about the same things.

- Now talk about things that might worry adults. Again, point out that adults worry about different things. Similarly point out that adults also worried about things when they were children. If appropriate, illustrate this with an example from your own childhood. Examples might be feeling worried about going to school for the first time or about trying a new activity.

- Look at the end of the story again. Daisy felt much better after she shared her worries with Grandpa. Talk about the benefits of sharing a worry with someone children know and trust.

- Look at the picture story. Discuss with children Levi's worries about going to the party. What is he worrying about? How does seeing his friend help him overcome his worries?

- Suggest that children draw pictures of people they would confide in if they felt worried.

Published in North America by Free Spirit Publishing Inc., Minneapolis, Minnesota, 2013.

Library of Congress Cataloging-in-Publication Data
Graves, Sue, 1950–
  But what if? / Sue Graves ; illustrated by Desideria Guicciardini.
     pages cm. — (Our emotions and behavior)
  Audience: Age 4 to 8.
  ISBN-13: 978-1-57542-444-6
  ISBN-10: 1-57542-444-4
  1. Worry in children—Juvenile literature. I. Guicciardini, Desideria,
illustrator. II. Title.
  BF575.W8G73 2013
  152.4'6–dc23
                                        2013012337

Reading Level Grade 1; Interest Level Ages 4–8; Fountas & Pinnell Guided Reading Level I

10 9 8 7 6 5 4 3 2 1
Printed in China
S14100513

Free Spirit Publishing Inc.
Minneapolis, MN
(612) 338-2068
help4kids@freespirit.com
www.freespirit.com

First published in 2013 by Franklin Watts, a division of Hachette Children's Books • London, UK, and Sydney, Australia

Text © Franklin Watts 2013
Illustrations © Desideria Guicciardini 2013

Editor: Jackie Hamley
Designer: Peter Scoulding